The HAUNTED SCHOOL

Caroline Rose
Illustrations by Mike Dorey

BARRON'S

Ping! An eraser bounced off Miss Barlow's desk, and whizzed past her ear. "Who threw that?" she shrieked. The class sat in silence. No one had thrown the eraser, just as no one was holding the large woolen glove that even now was flapping about and pointing at something outside the window. It seemed to be awfully excited.

"It has to be one of you!" insisted Miss Barlow, looking cross. "Really, Miss Barlow, it isn't us!" exclaimed _____ . "It's not our fault that the school's haunted. We don't usually see it happen, but objects get moved about all the time."

"Don't expect me to believe such nonsense!" bawled Miss Barlow. "But it's true!" pleaded _____ . "If we've lost something, it usually turns up on the table in the hall. That's how we know there's a ghost."

"It found my sneakers when they'd been thrown onto the roof," added a boy behind _____ . "It's a very kind ghost. You shouldn't hurt its feelings by not believing in it."

"THERE'S NO SUCH THING AS A GHOST!" snarled the furious Miss Barlow as a garbage can floated across the room and emptied itself on her feet. "I won't put up with these tricks! And, if the person who is fooling around doesn't come forward at once, I will punish the whole class! Ghost, indeed! What nonsense!"

The glove now left the window and made itself into a fist. It shook itself at Miss Barlow. She backed away. It pointed to the chair. Miss Barlow sat down. "All I can say is that I'm glad I'm leaving tomorrow," she growled. "I've had enough of this school."

"And we've had enough of you!" mumbled a girl at the back of the class. Luckily Miss Barlow did not hear that remark.

"What a day!" sighed _____ as they came out of school. "Thursdays are always bad, even without Miss Barlow," complained _____ . "At least on Fridays I have something better to think about than school. Why can't my 3-D comic book come out every day, and not just Fridays?"

"Let's go and see if it's in the store yet. Sometimes it comes in the evening before,"

suggested _____ .

_____ and _____ sauntered toward the store, passing two friends on the way. There had been construction outside the bank on the corner for the last few days. _____ and _____ stopped to look.

"They don't seem to have much interesting machinery," commented _____ . "They can't be doing anything very exciting."

"The hole's getting quite big now, all the same," added _____ as they peered into it. "Look how deep it is!"

A workman caught sight of them, stopped digging and waved his spade angrily. "KEEP AWAY! OFF YOU GO!" he yelled at _____ and _____ . "What's wrong?" asked _____ , puzzled. "We weren't going to fall in!"

By now, another workman was climbing out of the hole and coming toward them with a nasty look on his face.

"I think they mean it!" said _____ , pulling at _____ 's sleeve. "Let's go to the store."

"It's odd, you know," remarked _____ thoughtfully. "I can't see why they're digging a hole there anyway. That road was only resurfaced a couple of weeks ago."

"And there aren't any of the pipes and wires they usually have in holes," agreed _____ .

"No," added _____ , "just a lot of boxes. I wonder what's in them." "Maybe that ghostly glove was pointing at the hole when it flew around the classroom today," giggled _____ .

5

"And why were you two annoying the workmen yesterday?" demanded Miss Barlow furiously next morning, as soon as _____ and _____ arrived in the classroom.

"We were only looking down the hole," explained _____ .

"Don't you dare do that again! You're far too nosy," she spluttered, looking as if there was a lot more she could have said. The heavy book mysteriously hovering above her head seemed to worry her. The ghost was at it again. "Er…you can sit down now," she said.

"And it's nosy of her to fuss about what we do outside school," objected _____ in a low whisper as they went to their desks. "Everyone looks at road construction, and no one minds. Those workmen were as nasty as she is!"

"Even the ghost doesn't seem to like her," commented _____ .

They watched for a while as Miss Barlow tried, unsuccessfully, to grab the book that floated over her head. No one could understand what was going on.

"The ghost's never been like that with anyone else," said _____ . "Thank goodness today's her last day! There are times I think I'll burst if I have to stay in her class another minute!"

Fortunately, _____ and _____ didn't have to. The class was about to rehearse a play. Miss Barlow discovered, however, that a wooden sword was missing. Reluctantly, she agreed that _____ and _____ should go and look for it in the drama storage room.

Quick as a flash, _____ grabbed the 3-D magazine and glasses.

"Well done!" thought _____ . "Now we can look at the 3-D pictures while we're out of the classroom. That sword's bound to be hard to find. We can stay away for ages!"

"I had no idea there was so much stuff in the drama storage room! No wonder we're not usually allowed in," said _____ , falling over a box of wigs. "There's another glove like the one in the classroom yesterday. I'd recognize it anywhere!"

"It's strange that the ghost has suddenly started messing around," added _____ . "It's always been so helpful before."

_____ settled down on a comfortable pile of cloaks. "I want to read my magazine. You should have bought one for yourself. They only gave out glasses with the first issue, so I only got one pair. You can hunt for the sword!"

_____ found the sword in no time, so after that there was nothing to do. After all, there wasn't much point in trying on any costumes without a mirror to see the effect.

_____ tried looking at the magazine pictures without the 3-D glasses, but it was pointless—you needed them.

Glancing around, _____ noticed a picture on the wall. It showed an old-fashioned man with a large, hooked nose.

"Who's he?" asked _____ .

"That's Sherlock Holmes, of course," replied _____ . "He was a great detective, in books by Sir Arthur Conan Doyle, and much more clever than the police."

"He looks it," said _____ . "And that's a great hat he's wearing."

_____ now peered at Sherlock Holmes through the 3-D glasses. "Wicked! This is the only normal picture I've ever seen that can go 3-D!" shrieked _____ as Sherlock Holmes stepped out of his picture and spoke.

"I'd been hoping you'd come," the great detective said.

"It's 3-D glasses that make me come to life," Sherlock Holmes informed them.

"And your picture has suddenly gone blank in the middle," said _____ .

"I wish you'd tell me who you're talking to," complained _____ , puzzled at hearing a voice from nowhere. _____ passed over the glasses.

"Wowee!" exclaimed _____ .

"I have something important to tell you," said Holmes. "Your teacher, Miss Barlow, is a gangster. The workmen outside are also crooks. Their tunnel leads to the bank vaults. I've listened to them plot at night. They've even used this room to store the dynamite they need to blast the final wall."

"And the robbery is planned for tonight!"

"Hadn't you better tell the cops?" asked _____ .

"Only people who believe in ghosts and have 3-D glasses can see me," Holmes reminded them. "That's why I need your help."

"If they've used this room," said _____ , "they've probably left some evidence. Let's have a look." _____ was right. There, crumpled in the corner, lay a grubby piece of paper.

_____ unfolded it. It was a plan showing the course of the tunnel all the way to the bank!

The school janitor stuck his head around the storage room door. "Doe wud's supposed to be here," he sniffed through a handkerchief.

"Miss Barlow sent us," answered _____ , quickly hiding the comic book and 3-D glasses up a sleeve. "But she's a gangster, and we've got to contact the police!"

"Doe wud's supposed to be here. Dot thad I should be here byself with this cold. Id's gedding worse," he croaked.

"If you had come in here yesterday, you'd have found this room full of dynamite!" protested _____ .

"I'b dot id the bood for jokes," snuffled the janitor. "Can't you see I'b ill?"

"Yes, of course I can, but look at this plan!" insisted _____ . "It shows the tunnel they're going to use to rob the bank." Sherlock, back in the picture, was silently cheering them on.

"Go back to your class. I'b off to by bed." As he spoke, the janitor stuffed the plan into his pocket. Then he stumped off, herding _____ and _____ in front of him.

"Without that plan," wailed _____ , "the police will never believe us! I'm sorry, Sherlock! There's nothing we can do."

Next morning, _____ came as usual to call for _____ on the way to school, but _____ wasn't ready.

"If you don't hurry, we'll be late," complained _____ . "I'm not sure which teacher we'll be having now that Miss Barlow's left, but we don't want to get off to a bad start with a new one."

"Ssh!" _____ mumbled through a mouthful of breakfast, pointing to the TV screen. _____ hushed and listened.

"And now to local news. Accounts are coming through of a break-in at the Crest Bank," announced the reporter. "There has been a serious explosion there, but the police don't yet know how the gang made their entrance."

The television showed a picture of the bank. Dense, black smoke was coming from a broken window. The hole in the ground was also clearly to be seen, but there was no sign of the workmen.

"Isn't that the bank right by your school?" asked _____'s mother.

"Oh no!" cried _____ . "I've just realized! Those boxes in the hole must have been full of dynamite! No wonder the men were so angry!"

"Our evidence was there all the time!" exclaimed _____ . "And the hole must have been the entrance to a tunnel!"

"A clerk from the bank," continued the newscaster, "may have been taken hostage."

"There must be something we can do!" said _____ , grabbing a jacket, and making sure the 3-D glasses were in a pocket. "Come on! Let's go!"

"What about your second piece of toast?" called _____ 's mother. But the door had already slammed behind them both.

A large crowd stood on the sidewalk opposite the bank. The police had cordoned off the school until they could give it a safety inspection.

"There might be no school for weeks," remarked an optimistic boy.

"But what about the bank?" asked _____ urgently.

"Don't be silly!" laughed the friend. "We can't have school in the bank! All the windows are broken anyway!"

_____ and _____ pushed through the crowd toward the bald cop who was controlling everyone. "Have you found the tunnel yet?" _____ asked him. "And what tunnel might that be?" replied the policeman. Just then, another officer arrived. "We've found a tunnel!" he said. "It leads from the construction site straight into the bank vault.

Judging by the mess, the criminals must have used…"

"Dynamite!" put in _____ .

"You kids will be telling me next that you know where that missing bank clerk is!" retorted the officer.

"We might just have an idea," said _____ quietly. "And we'd better get to him fast. He might be hurt."

Unseen, _____ and _____ crawled, commando-fashion, to the back of the school. Luckily, the little lavatory window was unlocked, and they climbed in.

Rapidly, they made their way to the drama storage room. It was just as they had thought. The bank clerk lay there, his hands and feet tied, and a blindfold around his eyes.

"Where on earth am I?" he asked.

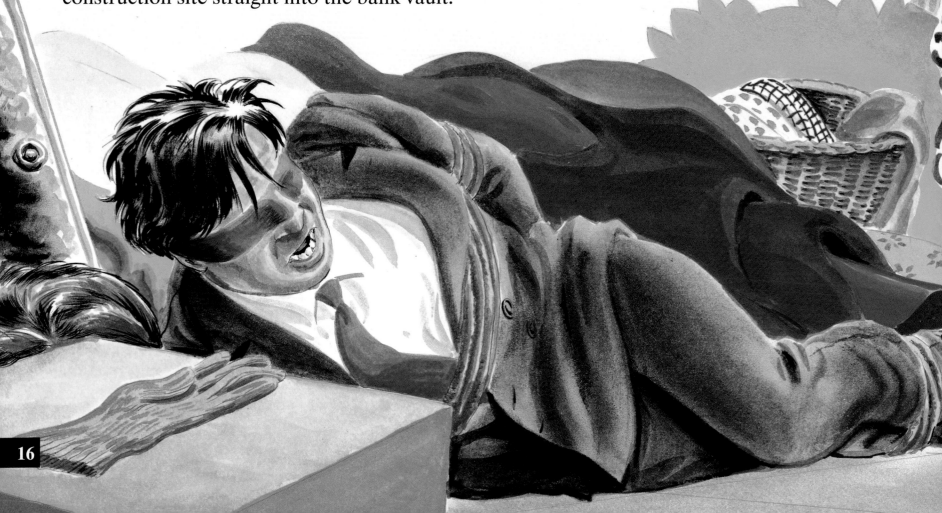

16

"Don't tell me you two are also part of the gang!" exclaimed the bank clerk. "How can you think that? We've come to rescue you!" said _____ indignantly. "Tell us what happened while we untie you."

The bank clerk explained that he had been working late but, strangely, the night security guard had not arrived. Then, at about eleven

18

o'clock, there was a terrible bang, and he went to investigate. The criminals were too busy to notice him at first, so he had time to see their faces. One of them was the security guard!

"And then some woman gave them the key to the school. So they brought me here. How did you know where to find me? It was a wonderful bit of detective work."

"We had the best detective in the world to help us," said _____ . "Would you like to meet him?"

"Greetings," said Sherlock Holmes, as the bank clerk peered through the 3-D glasses. "We must waste no more time if we are to catch the gang."

ading so fast that they could almost see through him, Sherlock Holmes led them back to the classroom, and pointed at _____ 's desk. "It's in there," he whispered.

_____ was embarrassed. The desk was in its usual mess, crammed full of pencils, comics, and candy wrappers. Any hopes that it might contain the loot from the robbery were dashed at once, as Sherlock Holmes pointed to a small, crumpled bit of paper. "What is it?" asked _____ , smoothing it out so that a few figures were now visible. _____ did not remember leaving anything like that in the desk.

"It's the phone number of the airport," explained Sherlock in a weak voice, "and it also shows the time of an overseas flight. I was listening when Miss Barlow called the airport and booked some tickets. She dropped the paper but I picked it up and hid it in your desk." Sherlock's voice was beginning to fail.

"She what?" asked _____ urgently.

"She's traveling… under a false name, and so are the men…" In an instant, Sherlock Holmes was gone and his voice had diminished from a whisper to nothing.

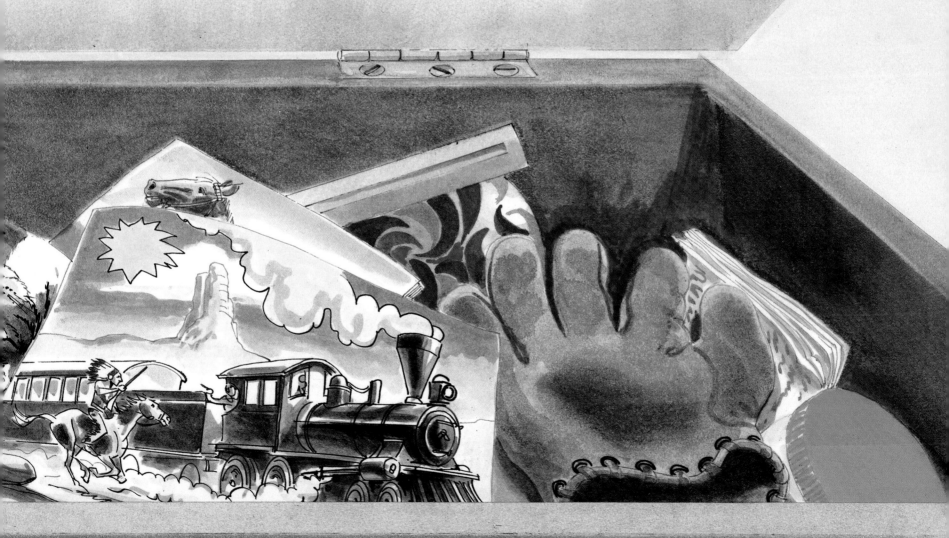

There was no time to react to the voices in the corridor outside the classroom. "You're under arrest!" an officer barked to the bank clerk. "I'm charging you with aiding and abetting the robbery at the bank last night. Our evidence shows that it had to be partly an inside job!"

"You've got the wrong man!" yelled _____ . "You ought to be looking for the night security guard."

"Not you two again!" exclaimed the bald cop as he entered the room.

_____ and _____ started to tell the officers all they knew, but did not mention Sherlock Holmes at all. The officers didn't look the types to believe in ghosts.

"Smart kids!" commented the bald cop. "I wish there was some more you could tell us."

22

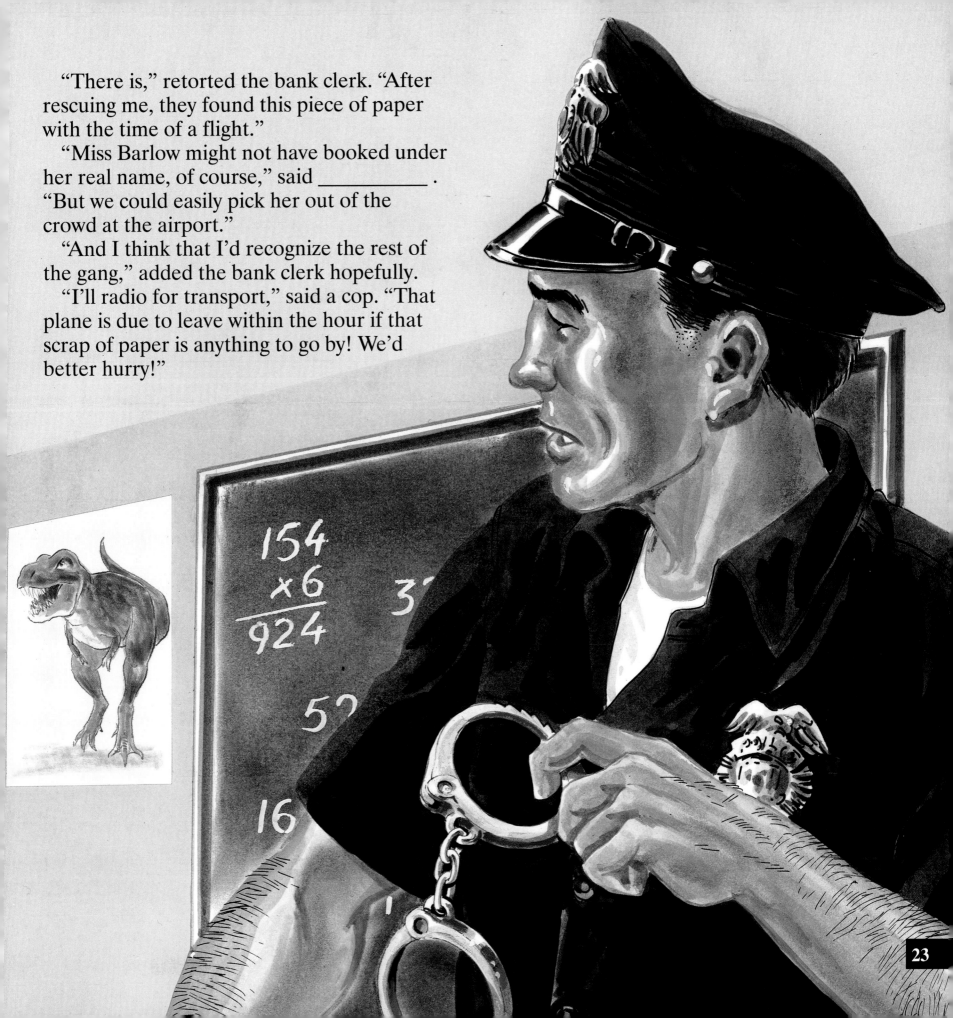

"There is," retorted the bank clerk. "After rescuing me, they found this piece of paper with the time of a flight."

"Miss Barlow might not have booked under her real name, of course," said _____ . "But we could easily pick her out of the crowd at the airport."

"And I think that I'd recognize the rest of the gang," added the bank clerk hopefully.

"I'll radio for transport," said a cop. "That plane is due to leave within the hour if that scrap of paper is anything to go by! We'd better hurry!"

The roaring sound was growing closer. "What's that noise?" asked _____ . "Your transport to the airport, of course," replied the bald cop.

_____ looked out of the window. A helicopter was about to land in the school yard. Over the school wall peered a hundred amazed faces. "Now I know how it feels to be a star!" crowed _____ .

_____ and _____ both began to feel queasy as the helicopter lurched upward. Their insides soon caught up with them, though, so that they were almost enjoying the ride by the time the helicopter reached the airport. It landed on the tarmac between two enormous planes.

"That's her!" screamed _____ above

the roar of engines. "She's wearing a wig and lots of padding as a disguise, but I'd recognize her anywhere!"

As Miss Barlow was about to board an airplane, she spotted the policemen and began to sprint toward a nearby car.

_____ and _____ dashed after her. Just as Miss Barlow's fingers touched the car door, _____ brought her to the ground with the tackle of a lifetime.

As _____ and _____ sat on Miss Barlow, they saw that the bank clerk had helped the police catch the rest of the gang. One of the gang was carrying a tuba, and the others had a drum and trumpet! They had disguised themselves as members of a brass band.

"Two of them are the men who were working on the road!" said _____ .

"And the other is the night security guard," added the bank clerk.

Miss Barlow beat her fists on the tarmac.

Amazingly, Miss Barlow maintained the whole thing was a huge mistake. Her passport said she was Miss Robawl, she pointed out; and she claimed that she was about to go on vacation.

"She's just mixed up the letters of her real name," objected _____ .

"She won't get away with it," said the bald cop. "But you and the bank clerk must still pick out the gang at a lineup."

"We'll manage!" said _____ confidently.

The three spent an afternoon inspecting row after row of sinister-looking people. Each time they recognized someone, they whispered to the bald cop. Soon they had identified the whole gang.

"So what?" sneered Miss Barlow. "An explosion would make far too much smoke and dust for that bank clerk to have seen anything properly. A good lawyer could show you have no real proof against us."

But the bank clerk smiled. "Haven't you

forgotten something?" he asked. "There's other evidence against you."

As he spoke, the janitor arrived with the plan showing the route of the tunnel to the bank. The fingerprints on it were all the evidence needed. "Dow you've got all de broof you deed!" the janitor mumbled crossly. His cold was still not better.

Later, the police found the stolen money stuffed up the tuba, and inside the drum and trumpet, too.

The bank manager gave orders for a splendid lunch at a grand restaurant. Lots of important people were invited to attend the occasion.

"Ask for anything you want!" said the bank manager generously, waving an arm at the piles of exotic food. There was caviar, and there was lobster bisque. There was salmon, and there were frog legs. There was also a side of venison.

"Could I just have pizza, please?" asked _____ .

"Me, too!" added _____ .

"Not a bad idea at all," agreed the bald cop. "I could put away several pizzas right now!"

The bank manager looked shocked. "It would be a pity not to give them what they really like," the bank clerk whispered.

The bank manager sighed. Then he smiled, and gave an order to the man at the door. Soon everyone was heading for the nearest pizza parlor. It was the best party any of them had been to for years.

But they all had to rush back to the Town Hall for the mayor to present a reward to _____ and _____ .

Photographers came from all the important newspapers to get shots of the ceremony. The pictures, though, might have looked better if _____ 's face had not been covered in tomato sauce, or the bald cop had not had a slice of pizza in his hand. The janitor's face could hardly be seen at all. He was blowing his nose at the time.

As soon as they could, _____ and _____ secretly went back to the drama storage room to thank Sherlock. He, after all, was the real hero. _____ looked at the portrait through the 3-D glasses. "I don't understand it!" said _____. "He's staying in the picture."

"He can't be!" protested _____.

"Here! Give me the glasses." But no matter how hard _____ and _____ stared or even squinted, the picture wouldn't come to life.

"It might just be that he's tired," suggested _____. "Maybe he's used up all his energy. Or perhaps he only became visible that time because he knew he had to."

"Could be…" agreed _____. "Let's tell him how we caught the criminals, though." So that is what they did.

"If only I could be sure he heard us," wished _____, taking one last look at the portrait through the 3-D glasses. About to turn away, _____ could have sworn that Sherlock gave them a wink.

All inquiries should be addressed to:
Barron's Educational Series, Inc.
250 Wireless Boulevard
Hauppauge, NY 11788-3917

ISBN 0-8120-6555-7

PRINTED IN HONG KONG
5678   9927   987654321